Library of Congress Catalog Card Number: 87-45762
Library of Congress Cataloging in Publication Data is available.

ISBN: 0-8050-0572-2

First American Edition

Printed in Hong Kong by South China Printing Company

10   9   8   7   6   5   4   3   2   1

ISBN 0-8050-0572-2

# The Man Who Wanted to Live Forever

Retold by Selina Hastings
Illustrated by Reg Cartwright

Henry Holt and Company · New York

There was once a man who wanted to live forever. His name was Bodkin, and his home was a small village which lay beside a river in a sheltered valley surrounded by green and gentle hills.

Bodkin enjoyed everything about his life. He was young, he was healthy, he loved his family and many friends, and he found the world a wonderful place.

One day he went to see the Wise Woman of the Village, who lived in a cave beside the river. "I want to live forever," Bodkin told her. "Can you tell me what I should do?"

"Difficult. Very difficult." The Wise Woman shook her head and stared down at her long black fingernails. "The only person who may be able to answer your question is the Old Man of the Forest. He is the oldest man I know, so old that he must have the secret of living forever."

So the following morning Bodkin set off along the road which led to the forest. Soon the dark green of the trees closed around him so that he felt as though the road led for many miles through a dark green tunnel.

Eventually Bodkin found the Old Man of the Forest seated on the trunk of a great pine. He settled down beside him. "Is it true, Old Man, that you will live forever?" he asked.

The Old Man of the Forest sighed. "I shall live," he replied, "until the last tree of all these trees is felled."

Bodkin was disappointed. "But one day all these trees *will* be felled, and then you *will* die, so that's no good to me. I want to live forever. Who can tell me how to do that?"

The Old Man sighed again. "Go and see the Old Man of the Lake. He is even older than I. He may be able to answer your question."

Bodkin found the Old Man of the Lake lying face down, drinking deeply from an immense expanse of water. "Is it true, Old Man," Bodkin asked, "that you will live forever?"

The Old Man of the Lake smiled a watery smile. "I shall live," he gurgled, "for as long as it takes me to drink this lake dry."

Bodkin looked anxious. "But one day the lake *will* be dry, and then you *will* die, so that's no good to me. I want to live forever. Who can tell me how to do that?"

The Old Man swallowed thirstily. "Go and see the Old Man of the Mountain. He is even older than I. He may be able to answer your question."

So Bodkin set off around the lake and across a barren, stony desert in search of the Old Man of the Mountain, whose castle, built of granite, sat on the highest peak of the highest mountain in the whole mountain range.

Bodkin toiled up the narrow path which took him first over gently sloping fields, then through a rocky landscape where tough little goats leapt from crag to crag above him, and finally to a region of great boulders covered in ice and snow.

The door of the castle was opened by the Old Man of the Mountain himself. "Welcome," he said. "I know why you have come, and I have the answer to your question. I shall live until this mountain stands no more!"

"That will do for me!" Bodkin exclaimed, satisfied at last. "I shall stay here with you, and this way I, too, will live until the mountain stands no more."

And so the two lived contentedly together for several hundred years – until one day, gazing out from the castle walls, Bodkin grew dissatisfied. He felt a longing to visit the village where he had been born.

"Don't go back," the Old Man begged him. "The village you knew has disappeared, and all your friends will have died long since."

But Bodkin was determined.

"I see your mind is made up," the Old Man said at last. "Take my horse. She is strong and swift, and will carry you there and back in a day. But," and suddenly he looked grave, "whatever happens, you must not leave the saddle. Only if you stay on your horse will you be safe."

Promising to do exactly as his friend advised, Bodkin mounted the horse and galloped fast as the wind – down the narrow mountain path, over the fields, across the desert, around the lake, through the dark green forest, and on to the road that led to his village in the valley.

There was the valley and there was the river, just as Bodkin remembered them.

But the village was now a great city, with a crisscross of streets lined with tall houses and strange signs, and crowded with faces unknown to Bodkin.

"What have I done," thought Bodkin. "This is not the life I used to know."

As dusk began to fall, he turned sadly back along the road he had come.

Suddenly, he saw ahead of him, a broken-down wagon drawn by an ancient horse. Its driver, an old man, sat helplessly beside it, his head in his hands. Dozens of pairs of worn-out shoes lay scattered over the road.

"Please help me, sir!" the old man cried as Bodkin approached. "My wagon has lost its wheel."

"I would like to help you," said Bodkin anxiously, "but I cannot. On no account may I dismount from my horse."

At this, the old man looked so despairing that Bodkin was moved to pity. Jumping down from the saddle, he heaved the wheel onto the axle.

The man began to thank Bodkin warmly. Bodkin paused, one foot already in the stirrup. A cloud passed over the rising moon and he felt a small chill at the back of his neck.

"Do not thank me. I was glad to be of help. But tell me, who are you and why do you carry this load of worn-out shoes?"

The old man smiled, and his eyes glistened greedily as he laid a soft hand on Bodkin's arm. "I am Death," he whispered. "And these are the shoes I have worn out running after you."

And with that he took Bodkin's arm and gently led him away.

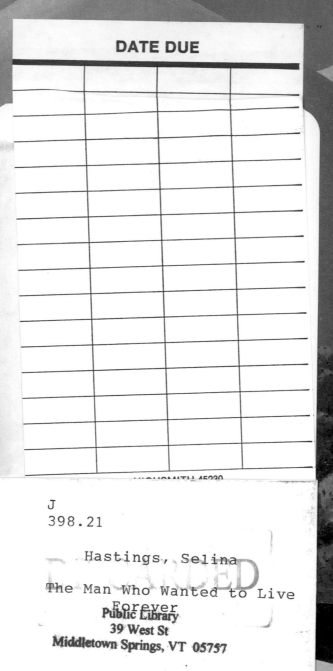